# SIDNEY

## The Little Blue Elephant

Sharon Rentta

# This is Sidney.

He's quite little for an elephant.

These are Sidney's friends . . .

Oscar,

Rufus,

Gloria,

Neville

and Betty.

They're even smaller than Sidney.
They play together all the time.

But there are some games
that Sidney likes . . .

Watch out!
He's coming down!

Steady on, dude!

while his friends aren't so sure.

And there are some games
that his friends like,

Erm . . . You go on.
I'll catch you up.

but Sidney isn't keen at all.

Come on, Sidney! Let's have a race!

The fact was, Sidney had a secret.
He didn't know how to ride a bicycle!
Bicycles are tricky, especially for elephants.

He was worried his friends might laugh at him,
so he decided to have a go while they weren't looking.

He just had to find his balance . . .

. . . and work out how to steer.

How hard could it be?

Help!

Crash!

Frank!

Oh, dear.

Oof!

Oh . . .                    Oh . . .

Oh, dear.

Meanwhile, Sidney's friends were having a lovely time.
But something was missing.
"I know!" shouted Rufus.

# "Where's Sidney?"

# They looked everywhere.

*I think he was here.*

*I'm sure he was here.*

*He was definitely here.*

# But where was he now?

He went thataway!

"Poor Sidney!" said Oscar. "What happened?"

"Riding a bicycle is really hard," sighed Sidney.
"Especially for elephants."

"Never mind," said his friends. "We'll help you."

And off they set!

Sidney never even noticed when, one by one by one . . .

# they all let go!

You're doing it, Sidney!

Yes!

Yay!

"Race you to the ice cream van!" said Sidney.
And guess who got there first?

"Riding a bicycle is easy
when you've got friends,"
said Sidney.

For my niece and nephew, Renata and Jason,
who are such fun to be around.

First published in 2009 by Alison Green Books
An imprint of Scholastic Children's Books
Euston House, 24 Eversholt Street
London NW1 1DB
A division of Scholastic Ltd
www.scholastic.co.uk
London ~ New York ~ Toronto ~ Sydney ~ Auckland
Mexico City ~ New Delhi ~ Hong Kong

HB ISBN: 978 0 439944 41 0
PB ISBN: 978 1 407105 94 9
Printed in Singapore

1 3 5 7 9 8 6 4 2

Papers used by Scholastic Children's Books are made from wood
grown in sustainable forests.